Movement In Moments

Kuldeep Sharma

Ukiyoto Publishing

All global publishing rights are held by

Ukiyoto Publishing

Published in 2022

Content Copyright © Kuldeep Sharma

ISBN 9789360169671

www.ukiyoto.com

To,
Humankind

Movement In Moments

Life moves from one moment to another. The duration of every moment may, however, vary. Sometimes, a moment feels like a decade, but sometimes, it flies in a split second. Some moments are to be cherished lifelong, whereas some moments are best forgotten. Just one movement of love can make the whole life well-lived. However, a moment of anger can render years of good relationships futile. But nothing is stays forever. Change is the only constant element, as moments keep moving from one to another.

The poems under the current heading depict situations pertaining to love, hatred, despair, courage, freedom, thoughts, feelings, and the divine. The poet has tried to convey the subtle meaning of love that sets one free instead of binding the lover and the loved one. In other poems, he has advises never to give up and keep walking towards one's goal, notwithstanding troubles and agony.

Contents

Keep Going

When the sea is unusually rough
You've got to stay strong and tough.

They wait for none, time and tide
If courageous, your luck you ride.

You have to defy all shocks of fate
Luck will smile at no distant date.

However gruelling, face your trial
You'll come out on top if you smile.

Enjoy the journey, accept your life
Sometimes bliss, at times with strife.

Not those get the most who most desire
But those whom failures never tire.

Just Be

If you are attached
Set yourself free.

If you want to be happy
Be as busy as a bee.

Love, Peace, and happiness
Things you need the most are three.

Don't expect others to follow you
People don't obey others' decree.

Every moment is temporary
It lasts only as does a wave of the sea!

Be ready to learn
Even when you grow as old as a tree.

Breathe, smile, and live now
Tomorrow, you can't foresee.

If you are in love
Just be.

Courage

There is no water.
Never mind!

There is no electricity either.
Does it still bother you?

There's no food again today.
We'll eat next time.

The old man died.
Man is mortal.

It's my birthday.
Time passes quickly.

There is a new government.
How nice!

But everything is the same.
Of course!

Will we ever live well?

We already do!

Will we ever be better off?

Of course!

Destiny

Every moment our fate is being created
Thoughts, feelings, attitude are related.

Our thoughts are shaping our destiny
Against our wish, they lead to a mutiny.

If our thoughts go back and forth
Our fortunes will not be much worth.

If we create our own thoughts
Our future will not be tied up in knots.

Rethink, reshape and alter your destiny
Watch your thoughts with great scrutiny.

Don't let everything intrude your mind
Look ahead and leave your grief behind.

Free Your Soul

When no one responds to your call
Walk alone.

Start enjoying solitude
There's no company better than your own.

When no one stands by you
Don't groan.

Don't open your old wounds
Let bygones be bygones.

Stones that people throw at you
Convert them into a milestone.

When no one claps for you
Be strong enough to be on your own.

When there seems to be no hope
There'll be a light to spur your soul on.

Be unique and break the monotone
Get out and claim your throne.

Freedom

It's like a cool breeze
Blue waters of the seas.

I am sitting on my knees
Accepted are all my pleas.

Something that nobody else sees
My heartbeats rise a few degrees.

I pamper her much and appease
To unlock bliss she has the keys.

Beaming through twilight trees
She puts my mind at ease.

The prolonged anxiety flees.
My soul is what she frees.

I Am Another You

You think
I discern.

you dream
I know.

You feel
I observe.

You say
I understand.

You smell
I taste.

You touch
I sense.

You hear
I analyse.

You see
I visualize.

You breathe
I live.

Paradox

Who hates you
Desires you.

Who avoids you
Wants your attention.

Who envies you
Wants to be like you.

Who criticizes you
Failed to become like you.

Who gossips about you
Is obsessed with you.

Who wants to forget you
Wants to get you.

Who hurts you
Loves you.

Perspective

It's raining.

The farmer is standing in his field.
I am drinking.
A young couple is walking.
The girls are dancing.
The boys are playing football.
They are stuck in a traffic jam.
The old lady is coughing loudly.
The ceiling is leaking.
They are sleeping under the bus shelter.

Spark In The Dark

When there seems no hope
There is always still scope.

If you have no friend
It's not yet your journey's end.

If you miss love and care
It's coming, don't despair.

When people doubt
Don't beat your brains out.

When you are tired
Recall what you have desired.

If you become frustrated
Don't become alienated.

When it's too dark
Look around for a spark.

Suspicion

He looked at me;
I got suspicious.

He walked towards me;
I walked away.

He walked after me;
I started to run.

He ran after me;
I stumbled.

He gave me a hand and said:
You have dropped your wallet!

Neighbours

What business is he into?

He just bought a new BMW.

He looks so arrogant!

He often throws parties.

He even owns a farm!

His wife looks stunning!

I see her often at the wine shop.

Even his daughter drinks.

Have you seen her boyfriend?

She comes home always late.

Is his son gay?

He wears a stud on his right ear!

What about this new family that just moved in?

Expressions

They express

Greed
by Benevolence.

Disrespect
by Courtesy.

Aggression
by Peace.

Apathy
by Compassion.

Jealousy
by Appreciation.

Hatred
by Smile.

Love
by Silence.

Seasonal

During your spring
They will cling.
For you, they will root
Committed firmly to the pursuit.

When you have no more leaves
No one grieves.
They do not remember
A has-been ever.

When the season changes again
You have their free rein.
Loyal, obedient, and caring
Who last time left you glaring.

You are the weather
Who keeps your folks together.
If you are not doing fine
You are an empty shrine.

Life And Strife

After a cry
Eyes are dry.

After the rain
The sky is plain.

As long as there is a desire
More and more you would require.

If you waste talent for greed
You would sow more and more weed.

After death
There is no more breath.

As long as there is life
You would never be free from strife.

Miracle

An obstacle
May lead you to a miracle.

There happened a miracle
When the time was critical.

Something could have been toxical
Didn't happen was a miracle.

Justice for a past debacle
May arrive as a miracle.

It may appear mystical
Loving someone is a miracle.

Taking a breath is a spectacle
Taking the second one is a miracle.

Be practical.
Expect a miracle.

The Healer

Love binds;
Hearts and minds.
Love unwinds;
It spellbinds.

Love frees you from hate;
Its only love that you create.
Love relieves you from the gloom;
Nature shows its beauty and bloom.

Love liberates you from fear;
You have your beloved's ear.
Love sets you free from rage;
It turns you into a little sage.

Love gives you wings
And makes lovers kings.
In Love, the soul is free;
There's glow, grace, and glee.

Harmony

My family lives in harmony
With me.

My wife likes the colours
I choose for her.
She loves to cook
What I eat.

My son likes to read the books
I recommend.
He loves the brands
I suggest.

My daughter loves the films
I take her to.
She loves the dresses
I get her.

They love the restaurants of my choice.
They love the music I listen to.

They love their friends I like.
They hate those I despise.

My family loves my choice.
We are a happy family.

A New Lesson

Just when you thought
The agony would lessen,
There   came some more
To teach you a new lesson.

Even the Supreme Lord Shiva
Had to drink the dreaded poison,
For your own soul's sake
Grow out of your mind's prison.

There will be more pain
There will be more treason,
This is a seed of the future
You'll grow in every season.

Contradictions

The sound of silence
Polishes diamonds.

The mind in the boiler room
Can be as silent as a tomb.

In the silence of the noise
It's the pause that annoys.

The death during life
Was a hero in strife.

During the prolonged hate
Love has a lot of weight.

Worry

Every life story
Has a chapter called worry.

When you worry
Things look twice as blurry.

Even when you worry
Problems go nowhere in a hurry.

If you just don't worry
you'll be free.

So don't cry, don't worry
Laugh and be merry.

Nature

The heroes have fallen.
The walls have crumbled.
In the new world order
Morals have crumpled.

The rogues are celebrated.
The wise have been humbled.
No more elegant and graceful
The angles look rumpled.

The earth has shaken.
The sky has trembled.
The seas have turned black.
Our thoughts are jumbled.

Ego, greed, and lust rule
Mankind has greatly fumbled.
Love and religion being traded
The human soul has stumbled.

Fear

Fear preys on the mind to conquer
If we keep calm, we grow stronger.

To meet my fortunes, I must endure
And not succumb to the bait's lure.

Don't let your troubles grind you
No matter what you have gone through.

You will shine after all defeat and regret,
You will forget your humiliation and sweat.

Do not ever give up
When you want it badly enough.

Align yourself with nature's design
It's absolute, profound, and divine.

Happiness

They are successful;
I am joyful.

They are on a vacation;
I am lying on the beach.

They are listening to music;
I am dancing.

There is a birthday in their family;
I am cutting the cake.

They are smiling;
I feel blessed.

They are in love;
I am in love.

Keep Walking

I walked.
I ran.
I climbed.
I stumbled.
I fell down.
I stopped.
I got up.
I walked again.
I ran again.
I climbed again.
I reached.

Don't Stop

Close your eyes
but not your heart.

Seal your lips
but not your mind.

Stop being hurt
but don't stop loving.

Stop being fooled
but don't stop forgiving.

Stop grieving
but don't stop dreaming.

Slow down
But don't say goodbye.

Friends

It's tough.
Don't worry.

Unbearable.
It'll be OK.

It will be OK I know.
Be strong until.

Need urgent help.
God is with you.

Can you help?
I just bought a new car!

Just this phase.
It will pass.

I wouldn't have asked.
Good luck.

Don't Quit

As long as you have family
Who you love insanely;
Trust your destiny blindly
When you see nothing yet really.

The bigger the quest
The tougher the test.
A hard trial you don't detest
Prove that you're the best.

Don't become bitter
If you have lost your glitter.
Things will get better;
Just don't be a quitter.

Even if life seems out of control
Soon you will be on a roll.
Diamond was earlier just coal;
Follow your goal with heart and soul.

Love

You touch
Not with hands.

I see
Not with eyes.

You say
Not with words.

I sing
Not with voice.

You smile
Not with lips.

I fly
Not with wings.

You think
Not with mind.

I am
Not without you.

Hey Time

Hey time;
You are treacherous!
You change all the time;
Sometimes with someone;
Other times with someone else!
Don't treat me as you are;
Treat me as I am!

Ambivalence

Sweet smile
A lot of guile.

Still waters
Deep quarters.

Sweet voice
Major vice.

Profound preaching
Acute leaching.

Extremely beautiful
Distinctly deceitful.

Deep silence
Immense impatience.

Highly religious
Very suspicious.

Be Different

In the air loaded with distrust
You must still dare to trust.

In a world filled with hatred
Discover your love sacred.

Even if they all spit atrocity
Someone would show generosity.

When they are consumed by anger
Be the anchor.

Among those who humiliate and hurt
Look for someone with a golden heart.

Bless them in their arrogance
Let your virtue be intelligence.

Dreams

A thought you nurture
Shapes your future.

Believe in your dream
It may be a divine scheme.

The distance travelled
Is the path levelled.

On the way, if you get tired
Buck up and get inspired.

Each difficulty you conquer
Makes you stronger.

If someone pulls you down
You are getting the crown.

Remain a gentle and pure soul
However high may be your goal.

Get Up

Fighting the crisis and insults
you grit your teeth.

It's a wonder that
you still know how to breathe.

At present
you have only misfortune to bequeath.

Stop moaning and mourning
get up from underneath.

Partners

Turbulent mind
Peaceful soul.

Prejudiced mind
Loveful soul.

Grieved mind
Healed soul.

Closed mind
Free soul.

Curious mind
Satiated soul.

Complaining mind
Thankful soul.

Loud mind
Silent soul.

Limited mind
Infinite soul.

The Winner

Having walked a thousand miles
My body is tired.
Having crossed oceans of time
My soul is inspired.

Having waited for so long
What I want is still desired.
My mind is wavering
But my time hasn't expired.

Patience and persistence pay
Even if a few attempts have misfired.
With each step nature conspires
In the end a winner is always admired.

Tomorrow

Is there still tomorrow?
Will it bring joy or sorrow?
If there's no tomorrow,
There's no time for sorrow.

How will be tomorrow?
Will I steal or will I borrow?
I have shed enough tears, I know;
I visualize now a better tomorrow.

Say hello to tomorrow;
Worries are like a poison arrow.
The water is indeed shallow;
Forget your pain and sorrow.

Faith creates a better tomorrow;
Hope heals your soul and morrow.
Fortunes will change, and you will grow;
To your cherished dream, you shall row.

We Won

You found me
When I lost myself.

You are the voice
When I want to speak.

You are the air
When I am out of breath.

You are the eyes
When I want to see

You are the light
When it is dark.

You are the nectar
When I am thirsty.

When I find none around
It's you who I surround.

Whispers

How the misery of the young wring
Bitter tears from the eyes fast aging!

That inward strife against the fearing;
The blasted hopes the death is guzzling!

The world shall be slowly recovering;
But won't get soon over the suffering!

But I can hear the luck softly whispering;
It's going to end, the human plundering.

You must know that out of human shuddering
Has often emerged the most beautiful spring.

Celebrating Womanhood

I see the wide horizon and I sigh;
I gaze at the stars with dreamy eyes.
The time is gone when I used to cry;
To climb I find no mountain too high.
Dreams that are staring me in the eye;
For them a thousand times one can die.
On the cozy bed of my dreams I lie;
I soar and float high in my own sky.
I can say today with pride as I fly;
Women hold up half the sky!

About the Author

Kuldeep Sharma

Kuldeep Sharma is a German language trainer and motivational speaker. He taught German at the Goethe Institute in New Delhi (Max Mueller Bhavan) for 15 years. He has been conducting German language courses and motivational workshops for the Indo-German Chamber of Commerce, among others. He has been writing poems and his own words of wisdom in Hindi, English and German for a long time. He has been on the editorial board of many educational institutions. Currently, he is writing his first book in English that deals with motivation and spirituality.